MW01092797

2X2=1
AND I'M DONE!

BY SHANEQUA DASHER

Books may be purchased in quantity and/ or special sales by contacting the publisher.

Mynd Matters Publishing
715 Peachtree Street NE
Suites 100 & 200
Atlanta, GA 30308
www.myndmatterspublishing.com

978-1-953307-09-5 (pbk)
978-1-953307-10-1 (hdcv)

FIRST EDITION

To all of the children in the world with big dreams and even bigger imaginations, especially my little dreamers, Kayla and Kyler.

CHAPTER *1*:
WELCOME TO 6TH GRADE

JOSIE WAS THE ULTIMATE CRAFTY FASHIONISTA.

SHE LOVED DESIGNING HER OWN CLOTHES AND CREATING DÉCOR FOR HER FIRST LOCKER. YOU NAME IT, JOSIE'S CRAFTED SOMETHING FOR IT.

SO IT WAS NO SURPRISE THAT WHEN HER NEW TEACHERS SENT EVERYONE HOME TO CREATE BOOK COVERS FOR THEIR TEXTBOOKS, JOSIE WENT ABOUT IT IN A GRAND FASHION.

SHE VISITED THE ART RESOURCE ROOM, GATHERED A FEW HELPFUL SUPPLIES, AND HURRIED HOME, EXCITED TO SHOW OFF HER NEW BOOK COVER DESIGNS BEFORE THEY WERE EVEN FINISHED.

WHEN JOSIE RETURNED TO SCHOOL THE NEXT DAY, ALL OF HER BOOKS HAD METICULOUSLY DESIGNED COVERS, EXPLODING WITH FABULOUS FLAIR.

WELL, EVERY BOOK BUT ONE...

HER FOURTH PERIOD MATH BOOK.

JOSIE HAD VERY STRONG OPINIONS ABOUT WHAT DID AND DID NOT DESERVE HER CREATIVITY, AND MATH WAS ONE OF THE SUBJECTS THAT DEFINITELY DID NOT.

YOU SEE, JOSIE DESPISED MATH. SHE THOUGHT IT WAS USELESS AND BELIEVED THE WORLD WAS TOO BEAUTIFUL TO BE BOGGED DOWN WITH NUMBERS AND CALCULATIONS.

"I MEAN, WHEN IN LIFE ARE WE ACTUALLY GOING TO MULTIPLY OR USE ALGEBRA? MATH IS ABOUT AS RELEVANT AS MY 6TH PERIOD WIFFLE BALL CLASS AND WHO ACTUALLY NEEDS WIFFLE BALL?" JOSIE THOUGHT TO HERSELF FINDING TRUE FRUSTRATION IN THINGS THAT DID NOT FEED HER CREATIVITY.

CHAPTER 2:
THE MATH-TASTROPHY

DURING HER FOURTH PERIOD MATH BLOCK, JOSIE ENTERED THE CLASSROOM ARM-IN-ARM WITH HER BEST FRIEND, JISELLE, AND DRAGGING HER LESS-THAN-FANCY BROWN PAPER BAG MATH BOOK ON THE GROUND BY A ROPE, LIKE A SICK DOG.

JISELLE WAS A MATH SUPER STAR AND ALWAYS SAT UP FRONT DURING CLASS. KNOWING HOW JOSIE FELT ABOUT MATH, JISELLE ENCOURAGED HER TO ALSO SIT UP FRONT, THINKING MAYBE SHE WOULD FINALLY GET SOME ENJOYMENT OUT OF THE CLASS.

JOSIE COMPLIED BUT MADE SURE SHE SAT ON THE CORNER OF THE SECOND ROW BEHIND BIG ROB, HOPING TO SOMEWHAT HIDE BEHIND HIS MARSHMALLOW FLUFF SIZED BODY.

WITH A MASTER PLAN IN MIND, JOSIE INSISTED THAT MATH WAS HER NAP TIME. SO SHE LAID DOWN HER HEAD AND BEGAN TO DOODLE IN HER NOTEBOOK UNTIL SHE FELL INTO A DEEP SLUMBER.

2X0 = 0
2X1 = 2
2X2 = __
2X3 = __
2X4 = __
2X5 = __
2X6 = __

13

"JOSIE?" MS. BENSON ABRUPTLY ASKED LOUD ENOUGH TO GET HER ATTENTION. "CAN YOU HELP ME SOLVE THIS PROBLEM PLEASE?"

JOSIE SLOWLY GOT UP FROM HER DESK WITH HER EYES HALF-CLOSED. WITH A BIG YAWN, SHE BELLOWED, "TWO TIMES TWO IS ONE. AND I'M DONE."

JOSIE MELTED BACK INTO HER SEAT AND THIS TIME, ADDED A LITTLE FLAIR TO HER STYLE BY REACHING INTO HER CROSSBODY PURSE TO RETRIEVE A PAIR OF BIG, BLACK SUNGLASSES TO HIDE HER NAP FACE.

MS. BENSON WAS FUMING, BUT DECIDED THAT NOW WASN'T THE TIME TO BICKER BACK AND FORTH WITH A STUDENT.

$2 \times 0 = 0$

$2 \times 1 = 2$

$2 \times 2 = \_\_$

$2 \times 3 = \_\_$

$2 \times 4 = \_\_$

$2 \times 5 = \_\_$

$2 \times 6 = \_\_$

$2 \times 7 = \_\_$

$2 \times 8 = \_\_$

$2 \times 9 = \_\_$

$2 \times 10 = \_\_$

$2 \times 11 = \_\_$

$2 \times 12 = \_\_$

THE BELL RANG AND IT WAS TIME FOR FIFTH PERIOD.

"ART! FINALLY!" JOSIE EXCLAIMED, READY TO LEAVE MATH CLASS. BUT HER EXCITEMENT WAS QUICKLY INTERRUPTED BY MS. BENSON'S STERN VOICE.

"NOT SO FAST, JOSIE," SHE INSISTED. "WE NEED TO CHAT."

JOSIE WALKED TOWARDS HER AS MS. BENSON CONTINUED.

"WHAT'S GOING ON WITH YOU? YOU SLEPT FOR NEARLY THE ENTIRE CLASS. ARE YOU HAVING A HARD TIME ADJUSTING TO SIXTH GRADE?"

TAKING A DEEP BREATH, JOSIE LET OUT A RELUCTANT SIGH.

"IT'S NOT THAT MS. BENSON. IT HAS NOTHING TO DO WITH YOU. I JUST REALLY DON'T LIKE MATH. I DON'T SEE THE POINT OF IT BEYOND SCHOOL."

"WELL, THERE'S GOT TO BE SOMETHING YOU ENJOY," MS. BENSON REPLIED
WITH A PUZZLED FACIAL EXPRESSION AND THEN ASKED,
"DON'T YOU KNOW HOW TO SEW?"

"YES, OF COURSE," JOSIE REPLIED SLIGHTLY CONFUSED, NOT FULLY
REALIZING HOW THE QUESTION RELATED TO THE CONVERSATION AT HAND.

"WELL, THE DRAMA CLUB'S COSTUME DEPARTMENT DESPERATELY NEEDS
HELP. ARE YOU FREE TO JOIN US THIS AFTERNOON? YOUR BEST FRIEND
JISELLE IS STARRING AS THE LEAD IN OUR NEW PRODUCTION, SO YOU'LL
BE ABLE TO DESIGN HER COSTUME AS A BONUS."

JOSIE WAS ECSTATIC. "YES! I'D LOVE TO JOIN!"

"GREAT! MEET US IN THE ART RESOURCE ROOM CONNECTED TO THE
THEATER AT THREE O'CLOCK," MS. BENSON INSTRUCTED.

EXCITED, JOSIE GRINNED FROM EAR TO EAR. "I KNOW EXACTLY WHERE
THAT IS, I'LL BE THERE!"

AFTER FALLING ASLEEP IN MATH CLASS, JOSIE FIGURED THE CONVERSATION WITH MS. BENSON WAS DESTINED TO GO IN A TOTALLY DIFFERENT DIRECTION. SHE NEVER IN A MILLION YEARS EXPECTED IT TO END BY BEING INVITED TO DO SOMETHING SHE TRULY LOVED DOING.

CHAPTER 3:
DRAMA TIME

AS THE FINAL SCHOOL BELL SOUNDED, JOSIE AND JISELLE LINKED ARMS AND SKIPPED OVER TO THE ART RESOURCE ROOM AND THEATER, RESPECTIVELY, FOR DRAMA CLUB. JISELLE WALKED ONTO THE STAGE TO BEGIN PRACTICE AND JOSIE CONVENED WITH THE COSTUME AND SET DESIGN TEAM TO BEGIN PLANNING FOR THEIR PRODUCTION OF "THE TEENAGE MERMAID."

MS. BENSON WALKED AROUND THE TABLE AND ASKED FOR THE TEAM'S ATTENTION.

"OKAY SQUAD, HERE'S OUR MISSION. BECAUSE THIS YEAR'S PRODUCTION IS "THE TEENAGE MERMAID," WE ARE GOING TO NEED LOTS OF WATER PROPS AND AT LEAST TWENTY MERMAID TAILS, QUICKLY. THE CAST HAS TO BE ABLE TO PRACTICE IN THEIR TAILS AS SOON AS POSSIBLE SINCE THEY WON'T BE ABLE TO WALK."

BEFORE MS. BENSON FINISHED GIVING INSTRUCTIONS, JOSIE WAS ALREADY WRAPPING UP A SKETCH. SHE HELD UP HER PAD AND SHOWED THE TEAM HER PLAN FOR A BEAUTIFULLY-DESIGNED MERMAID TAIL REVERSE HIGH LOW SKIRT.

"I ADDED PANTS UNDERNEATH SO EVERYONE CAN WALK AND DANCE FREELY."

"THIS IS GREAT!" MS. BENSON EXCLAIMED. "LET'S GET THE CONSTRUCTION PLANS FOR THIS UNDERWAY IMMEDIATELY. JOSIE, I'M GOING TO ALLOW YOU AND KAYLA TO TAKE THE LEAD ON THE COSTUME DESIGN AND THE REST OF THE TEAM WILL WRAP UP THE SET DESIGN."

JOSIE AND KAYLA GATHERED THEIR BELONGINGS TO BEGIN PLANNING.

"WOW, I LOVE YOUR DESIGN IDEA! MS. BENSON'S PLAN WAS TO HAVE EVERYONE WHEELED OUT ON STAGE ON A 'WATER WAGON' WITH A CLOSED MERMAID TAIL AND NO MOVEMENT. THIS MAKES SO MUCH MORE SENSE," KAYLA SAID TO JOSIE BEFORE THEY GOT STARTED.

JOSIE BLUSHED AS SHE REPLIED, "I APPRECIATE THAT KAYLA! COMING UP WITH CREATIVE DESIGNS FEELS SO NATURAL TO ME. I'M EXCITED TO GET STARTED!"

JOSIE CONTINUED, "SO, WE NEED TWENTY TAILS. I MADE ONE OF THESE LAST YEAR FOR HALLOWEEN AND I NEEDED ABOUT ONE AND A HALF TO TWO YARDS OF FABRIC FOR THE LENGTH AND FIN AT THE BOTTOM. SO, IF TWENTY PEOPLE NEED TWO YARDS OF FABRIC..."

JOSIE BEGAN TO WORK OUT THE PROBLEM ON HER SKETCH PAD.

20 PEOPLE X 2 YARDS OF FABRIC =

SIMULTANEOUSLY, JOSIE AND KAYLA EXCLAIMED, "WE'LL NEED 40 YARDS OF FABRIC!"

PLEASED TO HAVE COME TO THE SAME CONCLUSION, THEY SMILED AT ONE ANOTHER AND HIGH-FIVED.

"NOW, LET'S CHOOSE OUR FABRIC STYLE," SAID JOSIE.

JOSIE TRULY LOVED THE PROCESS AND PULLED OUT HER PHONE TO VIEW A LOCAL FABRIC STORE'S FABRIC PRICES.

"KAYLA, WHAT'S OUR BUDGET AGAIN?"

"MS. BENSON SAID WE HAVE ABOUT $250 FOR EVERYONE'S TAILS," KAYLA REPLIED.

JOSIE WAS IN DEEP THOUGHT AS SHE JOTTED DOWN A FEW PRICES.

"OKAY, THIS PRETTY SEQUIN FABRIC IS $10 PER YARD. THIS PLAIN COTTON FABRIC IS $4 PER YARD BUT WE'LL HAVE TO MAKE IT LOOK BETTER. THIS STRETCHY SUPER SHIMMER FABRIC, WHICH HAS THE PERFECT LOOK AND FEEL FOR THE STAGE, IS $6 PER YARD. HOW MUCH WOULD IT COST TO MAKE TAILS USING EACH OF THESE?"

IN A MATTER OF SECONDS, JOSIE CALCULATED THE TOTAL PRICE OF EACH FABRIC ON HER CLIPBOARD.

KAYLA WAS IMPRESSED WITH HOW QUICKLY JOSIE CALCULATED THEIR FABRIC NEEDS.

"YOU'RE AMAZING AT MATH!" SHE TOLD JOSIE.

"MATH?!" JOSIE RESPONDED CONFUSED. SHE WAS DOING WHAT CAME NATURALLY TO HER IN THE WORLD OF CREATING, NOT REALIZING IT HAD EVERYTHING TO DO WITH MATH. "I NEVER THOUGHT OF IT THAT WAY. I GUESS THIS IS MATH."

WITH THEIR FABRIC CHOICES IN HAND, JOSIE AND KAYLA WENT TO MS. BENSON TO SHOW HER THEIR COSTUME PRODUCTION PLAN AND BUDGET.

"GOOD JOB GIRLS," MS. BENSON SAID BEFORE INQUIRING, "WHO CAME UP WITH THESE NUMBERS?"

"I DID, MS. BENSON," JOSIE SAID PROUDLY. "I ACTUALLY REALIZED THAT WHEN I DESIGN CLOTHING AND CREATE MOST OF MY CRAFTS, I'M ACTUAL- LY USING MATH. I GUESS I JUST NEEDED TO REALIZE HOW USEFUL MATH WAS BEFORE I DISMISSED IT SO QUICKLY."

"I COMPLETELY UNDERSTAND JOSIE," MS. BENSON EMPATHIZED. "WHEN I WAS YOUR AGE, I FELT THE SAME WAY ABOUT MATH. IF YOU DON'T MIND, I'D LIKE TO TASK YOU WITH BEING BOTH THE LEAD COSTUME DESIGNER AND BUDGET MANAGER FOR COSTUMES AND PROPS. WOULD YOU LIKE TO HELP WITH THAT?"

WITHOUT HESITATION, JOSIE SHOUTED EXCITEDLY, "ABSOLUTELY!"

JOSIE WENT OVER TO A LARGE WHITE BOARD ON THE OPPOSITE SIDE OF THE RESOURCE ROOM AND WROTE DOWN THE CALCULATIONS FOR THE SIZES AND QUANTITIES NEEDED FOR THE SET AND COSTUMES. FOR ONCE, SHE FELT LIKE SHE WAS TRULY ADDING VALUE TO HELP OTHERS, AND FOR THE DRAMA CLUB, SHE WAS AN ABSOLUTE LIFE SAVER.

CHAPTER 4:
A NEW MATH-ITUDE

IN CLASS, JOSIE'S ATTITUDE ABOUT MATH QUICKLY TURNED AROUND. SIXTH GRADE NO LONGER FELT CLOUDY AROUND FOURTH PERIOD AND SHE EVEN DESIGNED A NEW BOOK COVER FOR HER MATH BOOK.

IN FACT, WHEN MS. BENSON ASKED JOSIE TO SOLVE A WORD PROBLEM IN CLASS, SHE WAS ACTUALLY AWAKE AND HER ANSWER HAD EVOLVED.

THE DRAMA DEPARTMENT NEEDS TO MAKE 2 MERMAID TAILS FOR THE LEAD CHARACTERS THAT REQUIRE 2 YARDS OF FABRIC EACH. HOW MANY YARDS OF FABRIC DOES THE DRAMA DEPARTMENT NEED?

"TWO TIMES TWO EQUALS FOUR AND I'M READY FOR SOME MORE!" JOSIE WAS SO EXCITED TO REDEEM HERSELF IN FRONT OF HER CLASSMATES.

THE MORE SHE EXERCISED HER PROBLEM-SOLVING MATH MUSCLE, THE BETTER SHE WAS ABLE TO PERFORM HER ROLE AS LEAD COSTUME DESIGNER AND BUDGET MANAGER. JOSIE WAS ON CLOUD NINE!

THE DRAMA DEPARTMENT NEEDS TO MAKE 2 MERMAID TAILS FOR THE LEAD CHARACTERS THAT REQUIRE 2 YARDS OF FABRIC EACH. HOW MANY YARDS OF FABRIC DOES THE DRAMA DEPARTMENT NEED?

CHAPTER 5:
THE GRAND FINALE

OPENING NIGHT HAD FINALLY ARRIVED. JOSIE MANAGED THE ENTRANCE, TOOK TICKETS, AND KEPT TRACK OF THE PROCEEDS FROM TICKET SALES. THEIR THEATER HELD A CAPACITY OF 500 AND 476 PEOPLE HAD ALREADY PACKED THE SEATS. THERE WAS A SCHOOL GROUP OF 22 STUDENTS AND 1 TEACHER OUTSIDE AND IT WAS UP TO JOSIE TO DETERMINE IF THERE WERE ENOUGH SEATS FOR THEM TO COME IN. SHE PULLED OUT HER SPECIAL NOTEPAD AND WORKED OUT THE MATH.

INDEED, THERE WAS ENOUGH SPACE FOR THE GROUP TO ENJOY THE SHOW!

AND AS THE OPENING ACT BEGAN, THERE WAS ONE SPECIAL SEAT LEFT FRONT AND CENTER FOR JOSIE TO ENJOY THE FRUITS OF HER HARD WORK. SHE SAT BACK, RELAXED, AND ENJOYED THE SHOW.

Now, you can join the Calculate and Create community!

Visit www.dashercreations.com to learn more.

CPSIA information can be obtained
at www.ICGtesting.com
Printed in the USA
LVHW080207121020
668549LV00015B/246